TIMES BEFORE CHRISTMAS
The Rhymes and the Reason

George F. Adams

Copyright 2019 © George Fulton Adams, New Lexington, Ohio.

Permission is granted to copy individual poems for personal use, provided that the author is credited.

ISBN 9781700574022

Preface

Eight-year-old Virginia O'Hanlon asked her father if there really is a Santa Claus. He suggested she write to *The Sun*, a New York City newspaper that he assured her would tell the truth. Francis Church, formerly a war correspondent during the Civil War, answered in the affirmative. In that reply, he wrote, "Nobody sees Santa Claus, but that is no sign that there is no Santa Claus. The most real things in the world are those that neither children nor men can see."

In Old Testament times, the rule was that no one could see God and live. There were exceptions, notably in Exodus 24:9-11, but it was still the rule.

One night that all changed. Some eastern scholars saw something new in the sky that told them a great king had been born in Israel. They went looking for him so they could honor him. As a result, the King of Israel sent people looking for him for a very different reason. On a hillside in Judea, some simple shepherds weren't looking for anything.

Being a shepherd in those days was about a low as you could go. They were uneducated. They were poor. They smelled bad. They were the first to see God in the form of a baby who was as poor as they were. For the next thirty-three years people would see Him – first as a baby, then as a child who could stump the experts, then as an itinerant teacher who worked miracles, then as a prisoner sentenced to die, and finally as the glorified Son of God ascending to the clouds to return to His Father.

And there were the angels. Literally messengers from God, angels may appear in whatever form suits the occasion.

Christmas is for children. We all know that. We all too often forget that we are children of God.

This book features nineteen poems that the author wrote as family Christmas greetings from the year 2001 to 2019. Mostly starring a little girl named Mamie (rhymes with Amy), they are not a literal chronicle of specific events, but are usually inspired by true stories. As a bonus at the end there is an upbeat poem that really does portray what was reality to a special group of children.

So try to read the following pages through the eyes of a child – a small child looking for Santa and at the same time a child of God looking for Santa's boss.

A Lamp for Our Feet - Christmas 2001

'Twas the night before Christmas, and all through the day
I'd been wondering how I would know what to say.

The letters were written, the stockings were hung,
The poems were read, and the carols were sung.

A sweet little girl had been put in
her bed,
With eyes full of wonder aglow in
her head.

She snuggled her doll and her big
fluffy cat.
Those eyes started closing, then
straight up she sat.

"Will Santa come, Daddy? I've
tried to be good!"
I smiled and I kissed her and told
her he would.

She settled back down with no reason to doubt,
So I turned off the light and walked quietly out.

I crept down the stairway and started to pace,
Then I sat by a window and stared into space.

The clock ticked so slowly and dragged out the time –
It seemed as if twelve o'clock never would chime.

Then just below Saturn I saw a red glow
That soon was reflected from rooftops below.

In less than a moment, that awesome display
Was revealing nine reindeer in front of a sleigh.

I wondered why Rudolph was leading this year
When the sky was not cloudy, but perfectly clear.

I sprang to my feet, but before I could rise,
The vision had vanished and gone from my eyes.

I guessed I'd dozed off – it was only a dream –
Then I heard on the roof every hoof of the team.

The chimney was shaking and ever so quick,
There, standing before me, was jolly Saint Nick.

He chuckled and asked, "Why your look of surprise?
Is this not the night that I ride through the skies?"

I stammered and said, "Yes, I know it's that night,
But I had some concern you might not make the flight,

"For I saw in a movie that you did some work
In a very large building somewhere in New York.

"On that September day when the towers came down,
I was fearful you might have been crushed to the ground."

He put a strong hand on my still trembling shoulder.
The look in his eye made me instantly bolder.

He said, "I was there, and I heard every shout
And knew all that went in to help others get out.

"I saw those who planned for the terrible day,
And I heard them exclaim they had gotten their way.

"They thought they had killed me, but that's nothing new –
They've tried for millennia now – at least two.

"You wonder why Rudolph is leading tonight,
With the sky crystal clear and the stars shining bright?

"When clouds hide the stars and the snowflakes are blowing,
I don't need a nightlight to see where I'm going.

"I know every chimney and roof in these parts;
The light's not for eyes – it's for minds and for hearts.

"For clouds of confusion and storms of defeat
Remind us we all need a lamp for our feet.

"The first time I carried a gift from afar,
I rode on a camel and followed a star."

I asked him, "Now, Santa, am I to assume
That a red-suited Wise Man brought gold and perfume?

"Am I to imagine a loud 'Ho, ho, ho!'
Amidst angel choruses?" Santa said, "No,

"I dressed very differently Christmases past,
Till that poem by Moore and some cartoons by Nast.

"You can buy a red suit and a wig and fake beard,
Then stuff in a pillow, but what's really weird

"Is that folks want to see me decked out in a store,
But they don't want to know what the season is for.

"I don't come at X-mas or Winter Vacation
Or Holiday Hoopla or Snowflake Sensation.

"I work for the Christ Child, and when he is there,
It may really be me in the white beard and hair.

"We hadn't been found in the classrooms of late
For we weren't to take part in affairs of the State.

"But those who brought on that atrocious attack
Instead of destroying us, brought us right back.

"For those who hate Christmas will never be heeded –
In fact, they're the reason that Christmas was needed."

He filled up the stockings; I climbed up the stair
And looked on the child who was sound asleep there.

I thought of a Christmas when I was her age,
When building bomb shelters at home was the rage.

I thought of a Christmas when she will be grown
And reading the story to babes of her own.

I wondered what perils they'll face, but I knew
There will always be Christmas and Santa Claus, too.

I leaned on her bed and I said a small prayer,
Then I heard Santa call as he took to the air,

"Remember this day is about Jesus' birth!
Merry Christmas to all, and to all, peace on Earth!"

The Kitten - Christmas 2002

Twas the night before Christmas, and out on the street,
A calico kitten had nothing to eat.

The holiday lights cast a festive warm glow,
But provided no heat to the pavement below.

The kitten felt drawn up the steps to the door
Where a little girl's cat had died hours before.

The girl saw the kitten and flew like a dart,
To give it a name and to give it her heart.

She gave it some food and a pan full of water.
I saw I had gained a new four-footed daughter.

They played and she squealed and it purred for a while,
Then it wobbled and slumped on the cold kitchen tile.

The kitten looked up and let out a loud cry.
She coaxed it to stand but it just wouldn't try.

She cuddled it close and made sure it was warm,
While the weather outside was becoming a storm.

She sang it to sleep and grew sleepy herself.
Then the next thing she saw was the Jolly Old Elf.

"Please don't think I'm naughty and leave now, Saint Nick!
I should be in my bed, but my kitten is sick."

He patted her head and he petted the cat,
Then pulled up a chair and beside them he sat.

"Come sit on my knee and I'll tell you a story
Of why we have Christmas in all of its glory.

"A long time ago it was past time for sleep,
But I had to stay up tending one hundred sheep.

"Most slept or ate grass with no cares or alarms,
But one sickly lamb lay in pain in my arms.

"The world seemed so dark as I gazed at the sky,
Till a star that I never had seen caught my eye.

"That star grew so large and its rays shone so bright
That it seemed it would make a new day out of night.

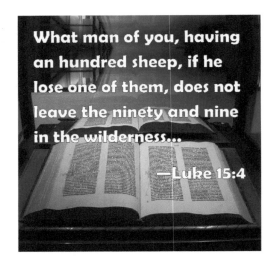

What man of you, having an hundred sheep, if he lose one of them, does not leave the ninety and nine in the wilderness...

—Luke 15:4

"I trembled with fear, wond'ring what could be wrong,
Then the heavens were filled with a glorious song.

"An angel appeared and said, 'Don't be afraid!
It's the birth of a King, and you'll see where He's laid.'

"Then the sky was ablaze with the heavenly host –
Twelve legions of angels from there to the coast.

"So I left all the sheep but the one that was dying,
And ran to the place where the angels were flying."

The girl asked, "Why didn't you ride in your sleigh?
The reindeer could fly with the angels that way!"

"Well, I was a shepherd back then," said St. Nick,
"My only equipment, a long crooked stick.

"The life of a shepherd was not very grand –
We were nearly the poorest in quite a poor land.

"We couldn't bring gifts like the Wise Men, you see,
But we were invited – admission was free.

"And, oh! What a sight! What a glorious sight!
A world full of darkness was suddenly bright.

"My sick little lamb grew so strong it was able
To leap from my arms and run into the stable.

"It ran past the angels, though I tried to catch it.
Its speed was so great that my legs couldn't match it.

"I knew it was sick and it might pose a danger,
But all fear was gone when I stood at the manger.

"I dropped to my knees and the Child touched my face,
Imparting a feeling of undying grace."

The girl said, "So that's when you turned into Santa,
With deer that can fly from the pole to Atlanta?"

"Not quite," he continued, "for we understood
Such an imperfect vision of that which was good.

"The power and peace that we thought we had gained
Seemed lost in a world in which evil still reigned.

"The glory and splendor of that wondrous night
Seemed almost forgotten by morning's first light.

"Before that new King would ascend to His throne,
He would suffer and die, all our sins to atone.

"We celebrate Christmas with glitter and gloss,
But we find the true gift at an old rugged cross."

Then he carried the girl and the
kitten to bed
And kissed them goodnight and
returned to his sled.

And I heard him exclaim as that
sled he did drive,
"Merry Christmas to all, and my
Lamb is alive!"

Historical Note:

The calico kitten in the poem was actually abandoned November 4, a few hours after the death of Mr. Kitty (the family cat who had welcomed two-day-old Mamie Adams home from the hospital on Fathers' Day 1998). The next day the kitten was brought to Mamie, who promptly named her Purry. The kitten turned out to be sick, but she helped a small child deal with a sad loss, just as that child made her feel loved until Purry also died two days after Thanksgiving.

Daddy's Home - Christmas 2003

'Twas the night before Christmas, and by the front door
A sweet little girl had been pacing the floor.

She'd take several steps... well, just make
that "a few"...
Then she'd pull back the shades with the
driveway in view.

Her daddy had left what seemed ages
before –
He had to stop bad guys.   (He called it
"the war.")

But soon he'd be home and she hoped
he'd come quick.
(They'd sent him home early, because she
was sick.)

She pulled up a chair as her small feet grew weary
And gazed at the lights till her vision was bleary.

When out on the lawn there arose such a sound
That she blinked and she squinted and looked all around.

She pressed to the door as she rose from the chair,
But she still couldn't see why a song filled the air.

From the back of the room came a soft "Ho, ho, ho!"
And she twirled around fast as her twirling could go.

Then she flew to Saint Nick in one hop and one leap
And said, "Santa, you only come when I'm asleep!"

"Well, don't be too sure, said the jolly old elf –
Sometimes when I'm there I don't look like myself.

"Just look at those angels out singing tonight.
You've seen them before making dark days more bright."

She looked out again and first one, then a few,
Then a large host of carolers came into view.

"Oh, Santa, you're silly! Those folks here to sing
Are people, not angels – not one has a wing."

"Not all angels fly," he said.   "Some do, of course,
But most drive a car or ride bikes or a horse.

"That one kissed your knee when you fell with a thud,
And those you've not met, but they've given you blood.

"A lot asked your mommy just what they could do
To give her a hand and help take care of you.

"So many gave money to buy you a gift
Or invent a new drug that will give you a lift.

"And each of those angels, because they all care,
Has asked for your comfort and healing in prayer."

She looked up and said, "Then I guess I don't know
Who's an angel from Heaven or lives here below."

"That's right," said Saint Nick, "The distinction is blurry,
But treat them the same and you've no cause to worry."

"Well, what about you?" she asked, tilting her head.
"Just how do you look when you're not dressed in red?"

"Now, that's a good question, and sometimes it's hard
Even when you've grown up; but now look in the yard!"

The choir of angels had vanished from sight,
And a taxi was driving off into the night.

A pair of large duffel bags
sprawled on the ground
As her father came up the
front steps in one bound.

She cried, "Daddy's
home!" and jumped into
his arms;
They forgot for one
moment all cares and
alarms.

Then she looked all around and said, "Santa was here!
And some angels were singing of joy and of cheer!

"Did you see them, Daddy? Which way did they go?
And where are they now, Daddy? Surely you know."

He laughed and said, "Well, I think you were asleep.
For it's late, though I know what strange hours you keep."

"Oh, no! It was real! They were all here tonight!"
He gave her a hug and said, "Maybe you're right."

For he thought he could hear a voice up in the sky:
"Merry Christmas to all, and please don't forget why."

Historical Note:

This photo was taken at a Christmas party in 2002.

Mamie's Daddy actually got home in April 2003. She was not waiting for him at home, but in the cancer ward of Children's Hospital. He was there in time for her first chemo treatment, on Good Friday. It was infused through the port-a-cath that was implanted in her side while he was en route from the Middle East. During her last year in this life she was absolutely convinced that he held her on his lap while the port was emplaced.

Her disease was officially in remission for Christmas that year, but she soon relapsed. Thanks to the many angels described in this poem, she would spend that and one more Christmas with her family.

He's Real - Christmas 2004

'Twas the night before Christmas, and all through the week
I'd noticed my girl was reluctant to speak.

She'd helped me put up the display in the yard
And deck all the halls (really decking them hard).

But she looked at the tree, and she looked at it long,
Without any smiles, so I asked what was wrong.

"Oh, Daddy, I'm sad. I'm so sad now because
A man on TV said there's no Santa Claus."

I laughed and said, "That's not a reason to care –
I've told you before, they say many things there

"That are far from the truth, and the networks all
know it.
But if they think people will watch it, they show it."

"I know that," she answered, "but this may be true,
For a big kid at school has been saying it, too."

"Then tell me – just who brings the toys and the cheer
All over the world on one day of the year?"

"Well, Daddy, they say that's why kids must be sleeping –
So we'll never see who it is that comes creeping.

"They say it's the mommies and daddies who bring
The dolls that can cry and the bears that can sing."

"So you think that your friends have it all figured out?
They know how it works, what it all is about?

"I'll tell you a story of children I met
On a cold Christmas Day I will never forget:

"They rode through the snow and they rode through the muck
And they rode to our camp in a big Army truck.

"Those kids were called orphans, and that's really sad -
Not one had a mommy, not one had a dad,

"But Santa arrived and that jolly old elf
Had a toy for each child and I saw it myself!

"When you see all the lights and you hear all the songs,
Don't you get a strange feeling of joy that prolongs?

"It goes beyond games and it goes beyond toys
It's magic for grownups – not just girls and boys.

"Old Scrooges who 'humbug' and shoo folks away
Will show up with smiles and warm greetings that day.

"And out in the trenches, where heads are kept low
And weapons are pointed to hold off the foe.

"A soldier would lay down his rifle and stand
For a bold Christmas walk right across No Man's Land.

"Then they'd fire not a shot, but embrace and shake hands.
(It's happened right here and in faraway lands.)

"A power so strong to make all that take place
Would cause fear and much trembling throughout earth and space!

"It had to be wrapped in a package that we,
In our human condition, could easily see.

14

"A human, like us, we can talk to but still
Who can hold a position no human could fill.

"Who walks on the earth and appears in the sky,
Who sees when we're sleeping and hears when we cry.

"Who shows up at Christmas, whose life is for giving.
As centuries pass he will still go on living."

She wrinkled her face and she raised her small hand,
And she said, "There's one thing that I don't understand.

"You told me the season's about Jesus' birth –
Not a man in a sleigh swiftly circling the earth."

"Now think, little angel, of what I have said,
And the words of all those who would see the man dead.

"Denying the premise, renaming the day,
They try to suppress it and take it away -

"That story so great we cannot comprehend
Of a gift far more precious than all we could spend."

Then the Spirit of Christmases
future and past
Was present before us, and told
us at last,

"I still do my work among
skeptics and fools
Who teach doubt on TV,
disbelief in the schools."

Then we heard him affirm as he
started to leave,
"Merry Christmas for all comes
to all who believe."

Through the Eyes of a Child - Christmas 2005

'Twas the night before Christmas, and all through the room
The lights bravely sparkled to fight off the gloom.

No laughter was heard and no footsteps ran wild,
There were no bumps or crashes to herald a child.

I thought of some Christmases long, long ago
When each brightly wrapped box was a magical show.

The paper was old - it had wrapped things before -
But the treasure it hid made it special once more.

And under the tree, scarcely able to breathe,
I'd examine each package throughout Christmas Eve -

Was it large? Was it small? Did it rattle when shook?
Was it soft like a sweater or dense like a book?

And where was that Santa? High up in the sky
Or hitching up reindeer still waiting to fly?

The sights and the sounds and the smells made it seem
Like a fairy tale coming alive in a dream.

The years flew by swiftly and, oh, what they cost!
I tried to hold on, but the magic was lost.

Then once again stardust like snowflakes did swirl
When I saw through the eyes of a sweet baby girl.

I'd hold her up close to a brilliant red ball
Or a shiny brass bell that was decking the hall;

She'd reach out and touch it and sometimes, you know,
She would grasp it and pull and not want to let go.

We'd ride around looking at cute figurines
And shimmering lights and Nativity scenes.

Each year she saw more, and together we learned
Of the joy we could share, and the magic returned.

We sang "Silent Night" and "Away in a Manger,"
Pursuing the hope and forgetting the danger.

But early this year, at an age not quite seven,
She took her last breath and she slipped into Heaven.

How can this be Christmas? Without her I fear
It can only be one more dark night of the year.

Then what through my tear-reddened eyes did I see
But that jolly old elf kindly smiling at me.

I told him, "Saint Nick, though your visit is pleasant,
There's nobody here that's expecting a present."

He answered me not with a loud "Ho, ho, ho!"
But he said, "I've brought news you'll be happy to know.

"I live at the North Pole. Yes, that much you knew,
But my work is assigned from a higher HQ.

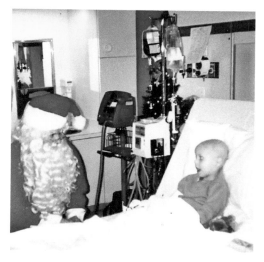

"I'm letting you in on the story I hear,
That her mansion was ready the previous year -

"Her work here was done and her time came to
leave,
But she loved you so much that you got a reprieve.

"Her scans showed remission two Christmases past –
That Yuletide together would not be your last.

"She stayed one more Christmas and helped you
prepare
For the time she'd go home where there's never a
care.

"You put plastic angels on top of your trees;
She's singing with real ones as loud as they please.

"Or sometimes your tree is adorned with a star;
She swings on the one wise men sought from afar.

"She asked me to tell you she's made you a gift,
For she knows you are sad and would give you lift.

"She always loved rainbows, and you know the sight
Is a promise from God things will turn out all right."

I smiled as I thought of the bow she'll display
When I'm caught in the gloom of an inclement day.

Then Santa saluted and turned to the door,
And I said, "I thought that's what the chimney was for!"

He rolled his bright eyes and he shook his old head.
"Well, I do it for kids, but it's something I dread."

As he swung the door shut and the lights caught the glass
They painted the wall in one glorious pass -

The colors were vivid and swept out an arc
In a room that had been so despairingly dark.

Then I heard a sweet voice as I pondered the sight:
"Merry Christmas, Dear Daddy! Please have a good night!"

<u>Historical Note:</u>
The most vivid and complete rainbow the author has ever seen appeared across the road the day after Mamie's funeral. Unable to capture it all in one photo, he had to make a composite picture.

The Kitty - Christmas 2006

'Twas the night before Christmas, and all I could see
Was a couple of packages under the tree.

I'd rise in the morning and pull off the wrapping,
Or maybe I'd wait till my afternoon's napping –

No need to be anxious, I knew what was there –
That one was to eat and the other to wear.

I tried to imagine my Christmases past.
The feelings I'd felt then - why couldn't they last?

The sun having set on the well-trampled snow,
I'd enter the house and the holiday glow.

I'd smell the warm cookies and smell the fresh pine.
I'd survey the gifts, counting those that were mine,

Admiring the tree and the wreath on the door,
Arranging the Manger Scene figures once more.

Each moment was magic, each sight like a dream,
But that was a lifetime ago, it would seem.

Then what to my glistening eyes should appear
But my sweet little girl with her voice full of cheer?

"For Jesus's birthday I'll paint Him a kitty!
He'll wear a red bow! Daddy, won't it be pretty?"

I told her it would, and her personal touch
Would make Jesus so happy - He loves her so much.

She went right to work and her paintbrush did fly,
Making kitty and bow and a star in the sky.

Then came a small noise, just a thud or a thump,
But it startled me so that I nearly did jump.

My eyes felt all scratchy, my vision was blurred,
The scene that unfolded was, frankly, absurd:

The clock had sped forward with barely a tick,
And standing beside me was good old Saint Nick.

19

Then wiping the sleep from my eyes with a tear,
I told him, "Oh, Santa, my baby was here!

"I guess I dozed off and was dreaming a while."
"It was more than a dream," he replied with a smile.

He reached in his bag and pulled out a small gift,
Saying, "Here is a present to give you a lift."

But before I could reach for the package he bore,
He gave it a toss to the cat on the floor,

Who, driven insane by a catnippy vapor,
Then ripped at the ribbon and pawed at the paper,

While Santa explained that the whole Yuletide chorus
Means someday we'll see those who went on before us.

In no time the wrapping was nothing but shreds
And a mouse made of burlap was missing some threads.

The catnip fit ended; the kitty sat down
In the midst of the mess he had scattered around.

With green and gold scraps decorating his fur,
He looked at the toy and began a loud purr.

The laurel draped over his neck then to show
That he'd beaten that mouse was his present's red bow.

But then he looked up and held still as could be
And he stared at the star at the top of the tree.

After such a long gaze, when at last he did blink,
I tell you - I saw Santa give him a wink!

Then turning to leave he exclaimed one more thing –
"Merry Christmas to all, through the birth of our King!"`

With Jesus - Christmas 2007

'Twas the night before Christmas, and all through the land
Were stores that grew rich on a name they had banned,

While holiday music was borne on the breeze
From holiday parties with holiday trees.

I thought of the children who may never know
That the message of Christmas is not "Ho, ho, ho."

I was glad that my daughter had heard of Christ's birth -
Of how God had come down as a baby to Earth.

She knew and believed, and forever will share
The joy of His love and the peace of His care.

The day had been busy but all was complete.
She rested so still as I stood at her feet.

At bedtime we always had had a tradition:
She'd sleep if we sang – that was her one condition.

This night was too late – not a sound would she make,
And though I was singing, she would not awake.

I sang "Little Drummer Boy" straight from the heart
(Without "p'rum pum pums" though, for that was her part.)

Then "Away in a Manger" all the way through;
At last "Silent Night" - just three verses would do.

I placed a small toy from
a Happy Kids Meal
(A custom of ours that
makes Christmas seem
real.)

I dreamed of the
morning, that glad
Christmas Day
When she and these
others around her will
play.

On Jesus Christ's
birthday she'll share all
His joys
With all of those girls and
with all of those boys.

Though most of those children should long have been grown,
I knew they were not by the dates on their stones.

But dates have no meaning in Heaven above,
And we'll live there forever because of His love.

I gazed at the stars and I heard Him exclaim,
"Merry Christmas to all, and remember the name!"

Historical Note:
The inscription at the bottom of Mamie's stone is a direct quote.

She was attending children's church at Bicentennial Chapel on Redstone Arsenal. They were going to do a skit acting out the raising of Jairus's daughter. Mamie wanted to play the dead girl, but the teacher was squeamish about it because she had just been diagnosed with cancer. Mamie really wanted to, so the teacher let her.

In the midst of the mourning and carrying on, Mamie suddenly sat up and said, "Don't be sad, I'm with Jesus," and plopped back down in the dead position.

The Sleigh - Christmas 2008

'Twas the time before Christmas when, all through the day,
The children were focused on things in the sleigh.

They'd made stacks of checklists of things in demand
And special requests most would not understand.

From workshop to motor pool all of the elves
Dragged boxes and bags quite as big as themselves.

Then loading eventually came to a stop
(The rest on the lists were not made in that shop.)

Some elf engineers re-inspected the sled,
For instrument readings pegged out in the red.

The crew chief told Santa that, if he approved,
The rig was OK and was safe to be moved.

He'd have to sign there and initial right here
To waive the weight limit (again one more year).

He signed and he sighed with a soft "Ho, ho, ho –
I've got to get thin so more presents can go."

The loadmaster elf was all dripping with sweat –
The pressure was great, but he'd never failed yet.

He filled out a North Pole Form Six-Seven-Two
("List of Items for Christmas that Elves Cannot Do").

Then told his elf runner, "Go find the Old Man
And give him this paper as fast as you can!"

That form got to Santa with near-record speed –
Saint Nick bit his lip, for he knew what he'd read:

"My uncle is frightened and lonely tonight.
Please bring a new day with no bad guys to fight."

"My friend needs new drugs, and she needs them real quick –
The old ones stopped working and she's really sick."

"Sweet dreams for my Mommy and Daddy tonight.
They've been so sad lately. It doesn't seem right."

He folded the paper and fought back a tear,
Then climbed in the sleigh and called out to the deer.

"Now Dasher, now Dancer, now Rudolph and all!
We've got to look sharp and we've got to stand tall."

And soon to the children the sleigh did appear.
They started to giggle, then let out a cheer.

They swarmed all around and they handled
the toys,
The games, books, and clothes for the good
girls and boys.

At last they had finished inspecting the load,
And shouted to Santa, "It's great! Hit the
road!"

He straightened his hat, brushed the snow off one boot,
Then turned and gave Jesus a snappy salute.

The team dashed away on a heading for Earth
While the children lit candles to mark Jesus' birth.

And they heard Him exclaim as He blew them all out,
"I wish my world knew what this season's about!"

The Story - Christmas 2009

'Twas the night before Christmas, and all 'round the tree,
The children were playing and singing with glee.

They danced and they laughed and they squealed with delight,
For Christmas would come at the end of that night.

Then one little girl climbed up on one strong knee
And said, "Tell me a story! Please tell one to me!"

"The one of why Santa Claus flies through the sky
Taking presents to children! Oh, please tell me why!"

The children stopped playing and all gathered near,
For the sound of that voice is a wonder to hear.

"It's been many years – twenty hundred at least –
Since wise men were studying stars in the east,

"When what to their wondering eyes should appear
But a star with a promise of hope and good cheer!

"They set out at once on a journey so far,
Drawn by the promise and led by the star.

"A King had been born of course - that much they knew,
So they asked old King Herod, who had not a clue.

"But the scribes did their homework and sent them away
To Bethlehem's village, their tribute to pay.

"Now here are the gifts that those wise men did bring –
Frankincense for the Priest and some gold for the King,

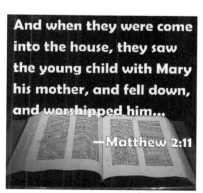

And when they were come into the house, they saw the young child with Mary his mother, and fell down, and worshipped him...

—Matthew 2:11

"Myrrh for the Sacrifice, perfect and true –
Together they symbolize God's gift to you.

"I was born as a frail little baby like you;
Like you, I was helpless but, like you, I grew.

"I played and I sang and I laughed and I cried,
And, like you, I suffered and, like you, I died.

"The Father sent me, and when it was my turn,
I gave you my life for what you could not earn.

"So Christmas is giving and Christmas is love
And Christmas is joy to the world from above.

"Then who is the person called Jolly Saint Nick?
A part of the spirit or simply a trick?

"A man who loves children and never will die,
Who comes with an escort of beasts that can fly,

"Who gladdens small hearts in the still of the night –
Now what do you think? Does that sound about right?"

She sat for a moment and thought for a while,
Then lifted her head and announced with a smile,

"I think that some grown-ups have turned things around –
They've got it all backwards and turned upside down!

"In a red or green suit, as a fat man or slim,
Santa doesn't make Christmas. No, Christmas makes him!"

Then the Christmas Star twinkled in code through its light,
"Merry Christmas to all, and to all a good night."

The Letter - Christmas 2010

'Twas the night before Christmas and all through my nook
Not a corner or wall had a holiday look.

I had lots of boxes of tinsel and lights –
The stuff that should brighten the pre-Christmas nights,

But I didn't feel up to creating displays
In these long winter nights or these short winter days.

I thought of a song that the Man in Black sang
Of some bells he had heard and the message they rang.

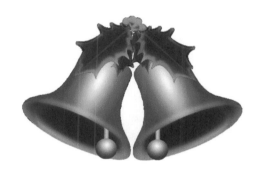

They'd rung it so long, they were ringing it still,
They rang about peace and they rang of good will,

But the singer replied, as he bowed in despair,
That war and injustice and hate filled the air.

Those words had been penned generations before,
When our country was torn by a great Civil War,

But I thought as I pondered the song's second verse,
"Things have gotten no better - they're still getting worse."

And though the bells countered the whiner's mistake
And pealed loud and deep, "God's alive and awake,"

I thought, "That sounds pretty, but who would be fooled?
For who can recall when the wrong hasn't ruled?"

Then, suddenly startled right out of my gloom,
I saw I was not all alone in my room.

A man dressed in red and disguised with a beard
Would soon fill his bag with my TV, I feared.

He pulled out a paper and gave it to me
And said, "Here is a letter I want you to see."

The printing I knew from a time now gone by
(All caps, but with circles to dot every "I").

I asked, "Where'd you get this? What does it infer
When it says that her kitty is living with her?"

He answered, "Your little girl wrote it today
And she gave it to me as I boarded my sleigh."

I looked at him harshly through eyes filled with tears
And said, "She's been dead now for over five years."

He said, "For this Christmas she wants you to know
That when Jesus came two thousand ten years ago

He came for one purpose, and one purpose only –
That those who are sad and are lost and are lonely

Can live on forever with those that they love,
With Jesus the Savior in Heaven above."

The next thing I knew I was rubbing
my eyes thinking,
"Wow! What a dream!" but there, to
my surprise,

Was the letter to Santa, right there on
the floor
At the end of some snow that was
tracked from the door.

As I dropped to my knees, I was sure
I could hear,
"Merry Christmas to all! Let its
meaning ring clear!"

The Picture - Christmas 2011

'Twas the night before Christmas, a quarter past ten,
But the festive bright lights found me gloomy again.

Some last-minute shoppers had rechecked their lists
And frantically searched for some presents they'd missed.

But most were at home or with someone who cared
Quite a lot for the season of joy that they shared.

I thought of the merrier Christmases past
When I had a small girl, but that time went so fast.

And I thought of the Yule Tides much longer ago
When I was the little one playing in snow.

Now I walked many streets, and I walked them alone
Till I picked out a park bench to rest my tired bones.

I gazed at a store window – oh, what a show!
But it couldn't bring back what I'd felt long ago.

And then to my wondering eyes did appear
A department store Santa, all bubbling with cheer.

He sat down beside me; I tucked in my chin,
As I braced for a gale force aroma of gin.

But all I could smell that had passed through his lips
Made me think of warm milk and, perhaps, chocolate chips.

I challenged, "Hey Santa! Is this not the night
You should be in your sleigh – maybe half through your flight?"

He said, "Yes, indeed, but the time zones, you see,
Make this hour an easy one – three quarters free.

"For I quickly found all of the stockings to fill
In the east half of Greenland and tip of Brazil."

I said, "Here's a dollar. Go get you a drink,
And just leave me alone here – I'm trying to think."

He crumpled that greenback; it "poofed" in the air.
In its place was a thermos of cocoa to share.

"OK! So you're good with your tricks and your magic.
Now leave me alone, lest I do something tragic."

He said, "No can do! I've a job here tonight.
I can't leave it undone. No, that wouldn't be right.

"I've brought you a picture. Look closely at that –
Note the nine-banded rainbow and fluffy white cat.

"And the name of the artist is clear, is it not?
See the capital 'I' with the circular dot?"

I cried, "Where'd you get this? And how did you see
Where I was? And what caused you to bring it to me?"

He laughed, "Ho, ho, ho!" and his belly did shake.
"I see when you're sleeping and know when you wake."

He chuckled and let out one more "Ho, ho, ho!"
And he said, "This was colored just hours ago

"At a grand birthday party where kids, all aglow,
Check over my sleigh and then send me below."

My strength was all gone and I fell to my knees;
As he vanished like snowflakes dispersed in the breeze.

But I thought I could hear – yes – I know I heard right:
"Merry Christmas to all, and to all a good night!"

The Seizure - Christmas 2012

'Twas the month before Christmas – November, you know,
The South had some sun and the North had some snow.

'Twas not quite Thanksgiving nor Veterans' Day,
Just a standard weekend, or it started that way.

But then came a siren and then came a stretcher
And then there were phone calls - some frantic, you betcha.

And off to the hospital, lickety split,
They carried my wife, who was having a fit.

Confined to a
wheelchair for nearly a decade,
From here to the doctor she's many a trek made.

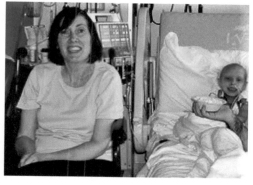

But now a brain lesion, or maybe a germ,
(Or neither of those – there's no way to confirm)

Sent neurons to firing much faster than lighting.
(They call it a seizure, and oh! It is frightening!)

They gave her strong drugs that stopped all her wild shaking,
But soon they predicted she'd never be waking.

They said we should plan on her going away –
It might be in weeks or might be in a day.

I asked, "Can she hear?" They said, "Always assume
That a comatose person hears all in the room."

We spoke of a child who is waiting to greet
Her and run hand-in-hand down a wide golden street.

(A child who once said, "When I've grown big and strong,
I'll push Mommy's wheelchair." But that turned out wrong.)

Another day passed. That day seemed like a year.
Until what to my wondering ears did I hear?

She had answered a question! A very weak "Yeah,"
But she'd answered my question and also my prayer.

Of course there were setbacks – pneumonia set in –
But first she spent Thanksgiving Day home with kin.

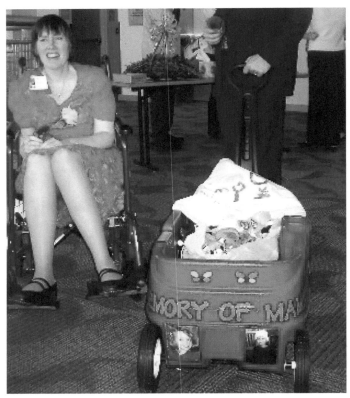

So Mamie will wait for her Mom (and her Dad),
And she won't grow impatient, or ever be sad.

No, she'll wait with the Christ Child.
How could there be tears?
(He's waited for all of us two thousand years.)

Though the first of December's still hours away,
And evening has barely put flight to the day,

I think I can hear midst the stars in the sky,
"Merry Christmas to all! We're not saying goodbye!"

Historical Notes:
Mamie's Mommy had been diagnosed with multiple sclerosis several years before. In early November 2012 she had a severe seizure. There is no way to know what caused it, but brain lesions and medications are two high risk factors that Debra had.

Donated wagons are so very important at children's hospitals for transporting them and their belongings in and around the facility. The occasion of this photo is the presentation of a wagon decorated by the children of Mamie's first grade class at Grace Lutheran School in Huntsville, Alabama.

Gone Commercial - Christmas 2013

'Twas the night before Christmas and all through the town,
I walked many streets, found a bench and sat down.

I looked and I listened, and all that I saw
Was so grossly commercial it stuck in my craw.

Then through all the tinsel and lights I could see
A department store Santa was headed toward me.

He spoke not a word as he sat by my side
Till I asked, "You big elf, are you well-satisfied?

This all is your fault, all this holiday stuff,
And the meaning of Christmas is lost in the fluff!

Just look at the glitter and lights that we've seen
Every night since the weekend before Halloween!"

Then Santa replied, "They're not nearly as bright
As the scene I remember on one Christmas night."

I thought, "He means lightning – a powerful storm –
He comes from a place where December is warm."

I asked him, "What happened to family time,
When we'd sit 'round the tree and the carols would chime?

From pole now to pole, from Tahiti to Rome,
Folks clog all the roads – hardly any stay home."

He said, "Yes, I know, and when some go away,
When they get where they're going, they've no place to stay,

Like the couple I knew who went traveling far
And gave birth to a son by the light of a star."

33

I mentioned the gifts bought with uncontrolled spending
And never a thought of the credit line ending.

"They buy costly clothes to be worn once a year
And give gifts no one needs just to outdo their
peers."

"Yes, gifts can be costly," old Saint Nick agreed,
"I remember some guys who brought strange
ones indeed.

"They wore jewels upon jewelry and gave a
small child
Expensive perfume and gold. Isn't that wild?"

I pointed and said, "You're the cause of this vice.
That list that you're checking – is EVERYONE nice?"

He said, "If I brought coal and switches to fools,
I wouldn't be welcome at all in most schools.

"I'm already banned in some places because
I represent Christmas, which violates laws.

"Yes, too many people forget what it means,
But sometimes a symbol packs more than is seen.

"And sometimes the truth is too big for our brains,
So we need something smaller that hints and explains.

"Think back on the folks before Jesus was born,
Expecting Messiah to save the forlorn.

Be not forgetful to entertain strangers: for thereby some have entertained angels unawares.
Hebrews 13:2

"What would they have thought if you told them that maybe
The Almighty God would come down as a baby?"

I lifted my head and he just wasn't there
But I thought I could hear his voice high in the air,

Saying, "Things are not always the way they appear.
Merry Christmas to all, and a blessed New Year!"

The Power - Christmas 2014

'Twas the night before Christmas and all through the park
The children had left, it was well after dark.

Looking up at the sky on that bright Christmas Eve,
I asked myself why (though I tried to believe)

Would a God who made Heaven, a God who made Earth,
Take the form of a man with a poor homeless birth?

They say He is God, but they say He's God's Son;
They say He's a spirit – He's three but He's One.

Though straining my brain, I could not understand.
Then a ragged young boy came by, kicking a can.

I said, "Santa won't come if you're not in your bed."
He answered, "Hey, mister, you're sick in the head.

"I'm thirteen years old, so don't feed me that lie
About reindeer that pull a big sled through the sky.

"While a short fat Saint Nick rings a bell over there,
And another, much taller, is in the town square."

I told him, "Our symbols are meant to reveal
What we can't see or touch, what we only can feel.

"Yes, Santa has helpers, we all know that's true,
But it shouldn't make Christmas less merry for you.

"The reason Saint Nick doesn't work all alone
Is so we can have roles to make Christmas our own.

"For Christmas has power, so many times more
Than the power of hurricanes driving on shore

"More power than all of the world's human hands
In love that no mere human brain understands.

"We're like a small bird lying hurt on the ground,
Afraid to be rescued, afraid to be found.

"The one who would save us so towers above us
We can't comprehend how that giant might love us.

"That power so awesome, so easy to fear,
Comes not in a whirlwind but pulled by some deer.

"That power so cosmic we can't understand
Comes wrapped in the skin and the clothes of a man –

"A jolly old man in a floppy red cap,
So we crouch not in fear but we sit on his lap.

"Oh, yes, it's a show, but a show can reveal
What we can't comprehend, what we're not sure is real.

"So Christmas is sleigh bells and tinsel and toys;
It mostly is love, but it's all of those joys.

"And the lights and the music say 'Christmas is here,
With power to fight off your sorrows and fears'. "

I ended my speech when a beam caught my eye
And I briefly looked up at a star in the sky.

Then I looked all around and the boy was not there,
It was like he had vanished just then in thin air.

And I heard a loud voice high up over the land,
"Merry Christmas to all, for you do understand."

Adopted – Christmas 2015

'Twas the week before Christmas and all through the town
The lights had gone up and the snow had come down.

A Salvation Army band tooted their horns
While a church bell pealed out that the Savior is born.

I thought of how Christmas had been bringing thrills
Since that star lit the night in the Judean hills.

I thought how I'd looked up through four-year-old eyes
For glimpses of reindeer who coursed through the skies.

I thought how that wondering view was revived
Through my little girl's vision when she was alive.

But then I decided the dream had grown old
And I might as well get home and out of the cold.

When out of the shadows a figure appeared –
A man dressed in red with a snowy white beard.

He said, "Ho, ho, ho!" and a few greetings more,
And exclaimed, "You're the one whom I've been looking for!"

I answered him quickly, not missing a beat,
"I already gave to the one down the street."

"Oh, no, it's not that, sir – I just need a hand
To look after my reindeer. (They're skittish on land.)"

"Oh, come now! It's easy to rent a red suit,
But you claim you're equipped with some reindeer, to boot?"

He whistled and called out, "Now Rudolph, let's go!"
And directed my gaze to a bobbing red glow.

"I'm off to a party, and while I am gone
Those critters would scatter both hither and yon."

I asked, "If they're that quick to take to the hoof,
What makes them stay put Christmas Eve on a roof?"

He said, "You could figure that out for yourself –
That night I bring Tex, the old reindeer-hand elf.

"But most of December is busy, you see,
So the workshop can't spare him to come down with me."

I said, "Well, look here. I have somewhere to go,"
But the big guy just vanished in flurries of snow.

And before I could blink he was true to his word –
Sheer chaos broke out in that nine-reindeer herd.

They nibbled on wreaths and they strayed in the street.
When Santa got back I was thoroughly beat.

He just whistled his whistle and chuckled, "Fall in!"
And they formed in a line just as straight as a pin.

I said, "You do magic, I have to admit,
So why did you need me? Just where do I fit?"

He answered, "I don't have the power, you see;
I don't make the magic. The magic makes me.

"You can hang up your lights and sing songs till you're
blue,
But all that won't bring Christmas magic to you.

"That magic came two thousand long years ago
From the One who makes starlight, the One who
makes snow."

He smiled and he told me, "The party's not through –
The kids are still there and they're waiting for you."

I said, "I'm too busy. I can't go. No way."
But, the next thing I knew, I was up in the sleigh.

I soon was surrounded by children who chattered.
(I understood none of it, not that it mattered.)

They showed me their toys and the pictures they drew.
They showed me their goodies, and shared with me, too.

They asked if I have any children at home
And if they are little or if they are grown.

I told them, "My little girl lives up in Heaven
For Christmas with Jesus since she was just seven."

"But you still have us!" affirmed one little girl.
Then the three oldest kids moved aside in a whirl.

And when they returned from their little powwow
They announced, "You're adopted. You're one of us now."

Adoption Ring Leaders

They all gave me hugs, then we sang "Silent Night"
As we stood round the tree that was lit up so bright.

And I heard through the laughter of girls and of boys,
"Merry Christmas to all, not just kids with new toys."

Historical Note:

Although it didn't really happen at Christmas time, "Doctor" Payton, "Colonel" Carter, and "Princess" Miah at Cheryl's Learning Daycare really did come up with the idea to adopt the author on behalf of all the kids.

Times Before – Christmas 2016

'Twas the week before Christmas and all through the night,
I tossed in my bed, turning left and then right.

No vision of sugar plums, dancing or not.
No long winter's nap – not a wink had I got.

I counted the evils and ills of the day
And concluded tomorrow would be the same way.

I feared for the future and longed for the past.
I cried for the present, declining so fast.

Then from the front room a loud sound stopped my
brooding –
The sound was of someone (or something) intruding.

I reached for my gun and I jumped from my bed
And confronted a white-bearded man dressed in red.

I asked, "Are you Santa Claus? That can't be right –
You shouldn't be here, for this isn't your night!"

"You thought Christmas Eve? Not one second before?
Ho, ho, ho! No one waits for that day anymore!"

"But Santa! That blows the whole schedule away!
Your visit makes Christmas a magical day!"

He looked at me sadly, then led me away.
We climbed to the roof and we climbed in the sleigh.

He called to his reindeer and off we did go
Above all the housetops, above all the snow.

We went faster than fast as we flew through the night,
And I knew we were going much faster than light.

We soon saw the sun rise and, as you have guessed,
With time moving backwards, it rose in the west.

As the date on my watch rolled back year after year,
Sometimes we'd slow down so the view became clear.

We looked on a scene full of carnage and gore –
The land was ablaze and the world was at war.

We looked down at earthquakes and famines and floods,
At burning of buildings and shedding of blood.

My driver had changed some – his nose was all red
And smoke from a pipe swirled and circled his head.

(I guessed he had morphed to the Saint Nick of yore –
The cartoon of Nast and the poem of Moore.)

Then a stiff bishop's mitre sat high
on his head
And his coat became longer – a fine robe of red.

The sleigh slowed again, so I knew to look down.
My look of amazement changed back to a frown.

There were cities in filth, people living in dread,
And men pushing carts calling, "Bring out your dead."

I looked back at my driver and oh! What a sight!
His beard had turned brown and his robe had turned white.

But then he just vanished. My mind was at loss
Till I looked down and saw him there nailed to a cross.

As I stared down in horror at scenes there below,
The sleigh changed its shape and it started to glow.

I looked all around and then what did I see?
There were men riding camels and following me.

They told at a palace, "Now fine gifts we bring
To worship the Child who is born to be King."

The king wasn't joyful, but jealous instead.
And he ordered his soldiers to see the Child dead.

I saw a new mother with no place to stay
And a baby with nothing to lie on but hay.

Then quick as a flash I was back in my room –
My heart filled with sadness, my head filled with
gloom.

Then Santa said, "Listen. I see your concern
But think back on our journey – there's much you
should learn.

"Just look out the window. Now what do you see?
A cross on a steeple? A star on a tree?

"In spite of the bloodshed, in spite of the tears,
Those symbols stand out after two thousand years.

"Despite the cruel world and the heartache it gives,
The Babe in the Manger is with us – He lives.

"In ten thousand years – in a million years, too,
You'll be singing to Him who made Christmas and
you."

I felt kind of groggy, my eyes became dim.
Santa shrank till I couldn't see any of him.

But I heard from above as I nodded my head,
"Merry Christmas to all, because God is not dead!"

Snowballs – Christmas 2017

'Twas the day before Christmas and all through the store
I was looking for one thing – just one, nothing more.

But nothing was festive in that which I sought,
So it hid behind holiday hype to be bought.

You may say that I was a bit of a Grinch,
But that scene would make Whos throughout Whoville all flinch.

There were clerks dressed as Santa and clerks dressed as elves
And really strange shoppers who dressed as themselves.

They were grabbing at clothing and grabbing at toys.
They grabbed electronics to bring Christmas joys.

I gave up the search for the item I needed
And off to the exit in haste I proceeded,

Stepped out of the store and stepped into the snow.
The clouds were quite dark, so deep drifts soon would grow.

I used to enjoy this, but now that I'm older,
The snow seems so slipp'ry, the air seems much colder.

Oh, all of this Christmas stuff used to bring joy
When I was a happy-go-lucky young boy –

And then once again, yes, in fact even more
When I had a small girl to teach holiday lore.

But now I walked cursing the time of the year
Till a snowball whizzed past, barely missing my ear.

Why, that little rascal! No, wait – there are two!
I'll show them just what an old man still can do!

So I scooped up some snow and I packed it up tight
And I let the thing go then in subsonic flight.

Above the boys' heads was a snow-laden branch
Where my missile dislodged a cold, wet avalanche.

They had snow in their ears, they had snow in their eyes,
And I ran at them hard as they reeled in surprise.

But their mother looked out and she spoiled the fun –
She ran out the front door screaming, "What have you done?"

She helped me get up (not in very good form)
And said, "Sir, come inside to get dry and get warm!"

She sent those two boys to their room in a huff
And she gave me hot chocolate and cookies and stuff.

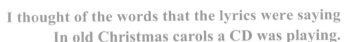

I looked at the lights shining
bright on the tree
And the tinsel as pretty as tinsel
can be.

I thought of the words that the lyrics were saying
In old Christmas carols a CD was playing.

I jumped up and said, "Ma'am, I've got to be going."
She said, "But you're wet and the wind's really blowing."

"I know, but there's something I really must do
And whether there's time... well, I haven't a clue."

I hurried on home and I looked through my junk.
I looked in some boxes, I looked in a trunk

Till I found an old wreath, not so green any more,
But it looked pretty good hanging up on my door.

And a star that was warped on a kind of a slant
Just fit on the top of a large potted plant.

It wasn't a lot, but I did deck the halls,
And I did it in time, before Santa Claus calls.

I found carols online and I started them streaming,
Leaned back my recliner and soon began dreaming –

I dreamed of a girl spending Christmas in Heaven.
(She'd spent them all there ever since she was seven.)

Above the dark clouds and beyond the bright moon,
A chorus of angels was singing a tune.

And what should my wondering brain hear and see
But that same little girl who was talking to me.

"Oh Daddy," she said, "it's so wonderful here
Where it's Christmas and Easter each day of the year!

"And Grandma and Grandpa are right here with me, plus
My kitty cat's here and he's purring to Jesus!"

Then my eyes opened wide when I heard a bold voice:
"Merry Christmas to all - you can have it by choice."

The Animals - Christmas 2018

'Twas the day before Christmas and all through the park
The lights were all lit, though it wasn't yet dark.

A squirrel scampered up and it stopped at my feet,
Looking up like he thought I had something to eat.

I said, "For a little guy, you sure are brave."
Then a voice from behind me said, "Rocky, behave!"

I turned toward the voice, where a big man appeared
With some long curly hair and a long curly beard.

He sat on the bench, to his knee gave a slap,
And that bushy-tailed rodent hopped up on his lap.

Then out of the bushes, all graceful and pretty,
In black and white stripes, came the wrong kind of kitty.

The man said, "Don't worry, you've nothing to fear,
For Stinky's not naughty this time of the year."

I said, "When I heard you address it as Stinky,
I thought of my little girl's kitty named Pinky."

"Yes, Pinky's with Mamie," he said with a
smile,
"Getting ready for Christmas in Heavenly
style."

Just then in the shadows I saw a few deer,
And two walked right up to us, showing no fear.

"Meet Flower and Lambie," the man said to me,
"And that one is Doc, over there by that tree."

I asked him, "Just how do wild animals know
You won't harm them? They all seem to take to
you so."

He said, "Years of practice in showing them love.
But you really can't learn it – it comes from above.

"It started one Christmas a long time ago,
When God's Gift came to Earth as a Child you should know.

46

"But now I must leave, for I work the night shift.
I've enjoyed our brief visit – It gave me a lift.

"Now Dash... I mean Doc, it's past time we should go.
And Blit... uh... Big Daddy, come on. Don't be slow."

It seemed they were gone in the blink of an eye,
As a bright shooting star made me look to the sky.

I guess I was swayed by the time of the year –
But a big bearded guy and a small herd of deer?

Did they all fly away? It was boggling my mind
Till Big Daddy walked by with two others behind.

I figured my magical thoughts were just silly –
The night was still dark and the wind was still chilly.

The world was still filled with the hatreds and fears
That plagued it for thousands and thousands of years.

Big Daddy

And yet that man knew that my girl's name was Mamie
(And even pronounced it right, rhyming with Amy).

Leo - The Lion

Regulus

He knew she's in Heaven (with Pinky, he said)
Where their glory outshines all the stars overhead.

The "King Star"
(named
Regulus), bright
and imperious,
      Never could
shine like the "Dog Star" (named Sirius).

Sirius

Canis Major -
The Big Dog

I gazed at the wondrous expanse of the sky
And the world here below, and I had to ask why,

Amid this and much more beyond what I could see,
Why God should take time to be mindful of me.

Then I heard a soft voice: "Merry Christmas to all –
To the weak and the strong, to the big and the small.

Historical Note:
The names you have read are true. Except for Mamie's kitty Pinky, all animal names were chosen by the children for actual wild animals seen near Cheryl's Learning Daycare.

The Wheelchair - Christmas 2019

'Twas the night before Christmas and out in the yard
I gazed at the sky and I gazed at it hard.

I longed to hear, "Look! Santa Claus has been here!"
But my girl's far away with her mother this year.

This time had been coming for quite a few years –
(Though a quick separation was foretold with tears.)

The doctors were wrong – yes, they made a mistake
When they said from a coma my wife would not wake.

The days became weeks, then a year, and then seven,
While our girl patiently waited and looked down from Heaven.

But wait, now I'm getting ahead of myself,
For there had been a time when they both
enjoyed health.

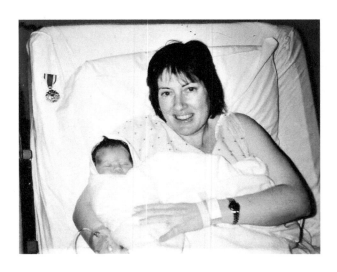

While our baby was small and not even a tot,
My wife began stumbling and falling a lot.

A trip to the doctor brought this diagnosis:
(It didn't sound good.) It was mult'ple
sclerosis.

Some drugs had come out only recently so
That the lesions were stopped; the disease
would not grow.

But the damage was done and the outlook was bleak,
For when muscles aren't used they grow ever more weak.

While that child learned to crawl, then to run and to talk,
Her mother grew weak till she barely could walk.

Our toddler grew tall and continued to thrive
Till she came down with cancer before she was five.

She had radiation and chemo and such.
She had operations – she went through so much.

The tumors were gone and that crisis had passed,
But we knew all along the good news might not last.

One day after church she said, "When I am strong
I'll push mommy's wheelchair." But something went wrong.

The cancer came back and it took her away.
So that show of her strength was for some future day.

Her mommy grew weaker with muscles unused
(Though the M.S. was dormant, for drugs were infused.)

Then one fateful Saturday, watching TV,
She had a bad seizure – as bad as could be.

That seizure robbed oxygen meant for the brain,
And she wouldn't recover, the doctors made plain.

They said she'd not wake, or at least not get stronger.
They said she had days, maybe weeks, but not longer.

But she opened her eyes and she saw and she spoke –
She even could laugh when I told her a joke.

She gave us some joys and she gave us some tears
As she lived here among us another six years.

Are there wheelchairs in Heaven? Most folks tell me, "No."
But our girl made a promise on Earth long ago.

If that little girl told an archangel, "Hurry
And bring me a wheelchair," the angel would scurry.

I tell you I'm sure – yes I haven't a doubt
That her mommy sat down and she pushed her about.

She pushed her, in keeping the promise she'd made,
Then they ran and they jumped and they climbed and they played.

So I'll wait on God's timing to take me away.
Merry Christmas to all, and to all a good day.

Debra Lee Adams went to live with Jesus and her little girl on February 3, 2019.

The Elves of Morgan County

'Twas the County of Morgan, in proud Buckeye Land,
Where two ornery elves tried to lend a wee hand.

The children were all just as pleased as could be
When they got their first look at the new Christmas tree.

But Teacher said, "There are some naughty old elves
Who aren't always nice or behaving themselves."

You must understand – their intentions were good
But they were too little to do as they should.

They knew that each child wasn't there every day,
So they thought and they thought till they thought of a way.

They figured each child could help trimming the tree
If each morning its branches were bare as could be.

So when all the stirring of creatures had stopped,
They un-decorated from bottom to top.

Those elves thought their pranks would be all in good fun,
But the kids knew they did what they ought not have done.

The children were mad when they looked on the scene,
And their colorful tree was now nothing but green.

They re-hung the ornaments nice as before,
But they disliked the thought of repeating that chore.

And those bad elves got bored with just un-decoration –
The mayhem got worse and became devastation.

The tree that stood straight with a Christmassy pride
One morning was tipped all the way on its side.

And even the star from the top of that tree
Had been taken and hidden where no one could see.

They had to do something – they had to act fast
To make that elf mischief a thing of the past.

So they got out some blocks and they built up a wall.
(It wasn't so high, but then elves aren't so tall.)

Star Found

String

You don't have much muscle when you are an elf
So you have to be smart to take care of yourself.

They came back that night and they looked at that wall
And decided it wasn't a problem at all.

They twisted a paperclip, tied on some string,
And had a small grappling hook ready to fling.

They flung it and flung it till finally by chance
It landed just right and was caught on a branch.

They climbed up that string and they climbed in the tree.
And soon it was just about ornament-free.

When elves become nervous, their little feet sweat;
When they think they're in trouble, their shoes become wet.

When children are sweaty, that sweat's filled with salt.
(That's just how sweat's made – it's nobody's fault.)

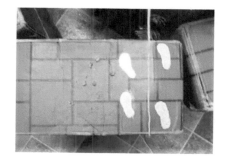

But not being children, elf bodies adjust.
Their sweat has no salt – no, it has fairy dust.

So if you believe there are really no elves,
Their footprints are there – you can see for yourselves.

But what elf had climbed it? Or had there been two?
A small jingle bell was the very first clue.

Climbing up or back down, or perhaps in a fall,
That bell had got caught in a crack in the wall.

Now elves can throw grappling hooks only so hard -
If the wall was built bigger, they'd miss by a yard.

So the kids fixed that wall and they fixed it up fast.
They fixed it up high, but it never would last.

They'd watched their cartoons and were ready for naps
When the wall tumbled down, nearly right in their laps.

They thought the elves pushed it, but that theory's wrong –
The bricks weren't stacked straight and the wall wasn't strong.

So maybe they needed to try something new.
Their wall wasn't working, but what could they do?

They racked their small brains, yes they racked and they racked.
They'd catch those bad elves – catch them right in the act.

So they went back to work and they stacked up the bricks,
But instead of brute force, they'd rely on some tricks.

For most of that wall was as high as before,
Except for one part that was almost a door.

The elves, being lazy, would climb at that spot
Where they'd step on Scotch tape and they'd stick and be caught.

When the kids checked their trap, they found only a shoe.
They'd not caught an elf, but they had one more clue.

This is what they are looking at.

Closeup of Shoe

They'd keep it as evidence, safe till the day
That Santa would visit. They'd see what he'd say.

They thought of a place where that shoe they could store
Behind a big heavy glass cabinet door.

The elves found it quickly (it wasn't well-hidden)
And used a toy tractor they never had ridden.

They hitched up a string
from the door to the tractor,
But, made out of plastic, its strength was a factor.

They revved up that tractor. It sputtered and coughed
And spun its big wheels until one wheel fell off.

The door was still closed, with the shoe safe inside,
But the kids knew it needed a new place to hide.

They put it up high, up so high on a shelf
That no one could reach it (at least not an elf).

But those
sneaky old
elves were
quite up to
the caper –
They made a
small
airplane by
folding some
paper.

They flew to that shelf and, as proud as a king,
They escaped to the floor by their grappling hook string.

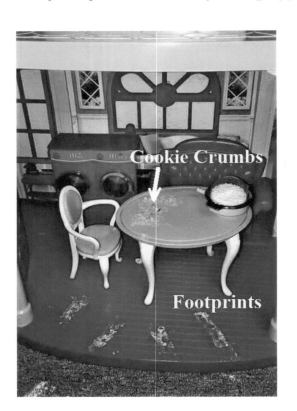

Cookie Crumbs

Footprints

Now bedtime
had passed and
they'd have to
go back
To the North
Pole, but first
they would stop for a snack.

The kids had come cookies, and hungry old
elves
Don't ask for permission – they just help
themselves.

They'd eat on the run, but then when they were
able,
They'd go to the doll house and eat at the table.

The kids were upset and were ready to fight
When they found that each cookie was missing
a bite.

They made a new trap at the scene of the crime,
At the spot where the wall was most easy to climb.

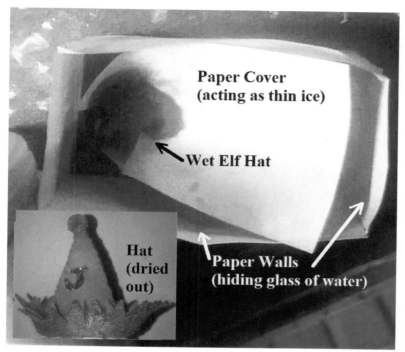

Paper Cover (acting as thin ice)

Wet Elf Hat

Hat (dried out)

Paper Walls (hiding glass of water)

They set up a glass and they filled it a little,
With just enough water to reach to the middle.

They covered the glass with a paper so thin
That elves who stepped on it would surely fall in.

They couldn't climb out. No, on that you could bet,
For both glasses and elves are too slippery when wet.

But something went wrong. (Yes, you should have guessed that.)
For all that was caught was a floating elf hat.

If they couldn't stop elves, they could talk to their boss,
For they'd soon have a visit from old Santa Claus.

He'd come to their party, and oh, what he'd hear!
Those elves would be sweating, with so much to fear.

He'd come to their daycare, they'd sit on his lap,
They'd tell him their dreams for that long winter's nap.

They'd tell him all that, then they'd tell him of elves
Who messed up their tree and their cookies and shelves.

We've had enough! We're going to tell Santa.

The Daycare Kids

Dear Elves

He'd hear all the evidence – all they could tell.
And they'd show him the hat and they'd show him the bell.

And that's how it happened. When Saint Nick appeared,
The kids were so happy, they shouted and cheered.

They gave him big
hugs and they made
their requests
And they told him
about their small
unwanted guests.

He thought of his
elves and compared
every angle
And knew in an
instant, "It's Jingle
and Jangle."

He said he would
talk to those two
naughty elves,
And he knew they'd
be sad and ashamed
of themselves.

Santa talked
to us and we
are sorry for
being ornery
elves. We left
you some cookies
to tell you how
sorry we are.
The Elves
Jingle and Jangle

So the very next day, when they checked on their tree,
The kids found an elf note, as nice as could be.

They said they were
sorry for not being
nice,
And they left some
fresh cookies (on
Santa's advice).

Now they're back at
the North Pole, but
some people say
That they fill in as
leprechauns Saint
Patrick's Day.

And this shall be a sign unto you;
Ye shall find the babe wrapped in swaddling clothes, lying in a manger.
Luke 2:12